THE DEAL OF A LIFETIME

& OTHER STORIES

The Deal of a Lifetime

*And Every Morning the Way Home
Gets Longer and Longer*

Sebastian and the Troll

FREDRIK BACKMAN

Translated by Alice Menzies & Vanja Vinter

PUBLISHED BY SIMON & SCHUSTER

New York   London   Toronto   Sydney   New Delhi

SIMON &
SCHUSTER
CANADA

Simon & Schuster Canada
A Division of Simon & Schuster, Inc.
166 King Street East, Suite 300
Toronto, Ontario M5A 1J3

This Simon & Schuster Canada edition November 2018

SIMON & SCHUSTER CANADA and colophon are registered trademarks of Simon & Schuster, Inc.

For information about special discounts for bulk purchases, please contact Simon & Schuster Special Sales at 1-800-268-3216 or CustomerService@simonandschuster.ca.

Library and Archives Canada Cataloguing in Publication

Backman, Fredrik, 1981–
[Short stories. Selections. English]
      The deal of a lifetime, and other stories / Fredrik Backman.
Translation of selected short stories by Fredrik Backman.
Issued also in print and electronic formats.
ISBN 978-1-982103-32-3 (hardcover).—ISBN 978-1-982103-33-0 (ebook)
      1. Backman, Fredrik, 1981– —Translations into English.
2. Short stories, Swedish—Translations into English. I. Title.
PT9877.12.A32A2 2018   839.73'8   C2018-902295-7
                                                 C2018-902296-5

Manufactured in the United States of America

10 9 8 7 6 5 4 3 2 1

ISBN 978-1-9821-0332-3
ISBN 978-1-9821-0333-0 (ebook)

THE DEAL
OF A LIFETIME

a novella

A few words before the rest of the words

This is a short story about what you would be prepared to sacrifice in order to save a life. If it was not only your future on the line, but also your past. Not only the places you are going, but the footprints you have left behind. If it was all of it, all of you, who would you give yourself up for?

I wrote this story late one night shortly before Christmas in 2016. My wife and children were sleeping a few arm lengths away. I was very tired; it had been a long and strange year, and I had been thinking a lot about the choices families make. Everyday, everywhere, we go down one road or another. We play around; we stay at home; we fall in love and fall asleep right next to each other. We discover we need someone to sweep us off our feet to realize what time really is.

So I tried to tell a story about that.

It was published in the local newspaper of my hometown, Helsingborg, in the southernmost part of Sweden. All the locations in the story are real—I went to school around the corner from the hospital, and the bar where the characters drink is owned and run by childhood friends of mine. I've gotten very drunk there on several occasions. If you're ever around Helsingborg, I highly recommend it.

I live six hundred kilometers farther north now, in Stockholm, with my family. So, in retrospect, I think this story was not just about how I felt about love and death that night I was sitting on the floor next to the bed my wife and our kids were sleeping in, but also about my feelings for the place where I grew up. Maybe all people have that feeling deep down, that your hometown is something you can never really escape, but can never really go home to, either. Because it's not home anymore. We're not trying to make peace with it. Not with the streets and bricks of it. Just with the person we were back then. And maybe forgive ourselves for everything we thought we would become and didn't.

Maybe you will find this to be a strange story, I don't know. It's not very long, so at least it will be over quickly in that case. But I hope my younger self would have read it and found it to be . . . well . . . not horrible. I think he and I could have gone for a beer. Talked about choices. I would have shown him pictures of my family and he would have said, "Alright. You did alright."

Anyway, this is the story. Thank you for taking the time to read it.

With love,

Fredrik Backman

Hi, it's your dad. You'll be waking up soon, it's Christmas Eve morning ... Helsingborg, and ... killed a pers... fa...

Hi. It's your dad. You'll be waking up soon, it's Christmas Eve morning in Helsingborg, and I've killed a person. That's not how fairy tales usually begin, I know. But I took a life. Does it make a difference if you know whose it was?

Maybe not. Most of us so desperately want to believe that every heart which stops beating is missed equally. If we're asked, "Are all lives worth the same?" the majority of us will reply with a resounding "Yes!" But only until someone points to a person we love and asks: "What about that life?"

Does it make a difference if I killed a good person? A loved person? A valuable life?

If it was a child?

She was five. I met her a week ago. There was a small red chair in the hospital TV room, it was hers. It wasn't red when she arrived, but she could see that it wanted to be. It took twenty-two boxes of crayons but that didn't matter, she could afford it, everyone here gave her crayons all the time. As though she could draw away her illness, color away the needles and the drugs. She knew that wasn't possible, of course, she was a smart kid, but she pretended for their sakes. So she spent her days drawing on paper, because it made all the adults happy. And at night, she colored in the chair. Because it really wanted to be red.

She had a soft toy, a rabbit. She called it "Babbit." When she first learned to speak, the adults thought she was calling it "Babbit" because she couldn't say "Rabbit." But she called it Babbit because Babbit was its name. That shouldn't be so hard to understand, really, even for an adult. Babbit got scared sometimes, and then it got to sit on the red chair. It might not be clinically proven that sitting on a red chair makes you less scared, but Babbit didn't know that.

The girl sat on the floor next to Babbit, patting its paw and telling it stories. One night, I was hidden around a corner in the corridor and I heard her say: "I'm going to die soon, Babbit. Everyone dies, it's just that most people will die in maybe a hundred thousand years but I might die already tomorrow." She added, in a whisper: "I hope it's not tomorrow."

Then she suddenly looked up in fear, glanced around as though she had heard footsteps in the corridor. She quickly grabbed Babbit and whispered good night to the red chair. "It's her! She's coming!" the girl hissed, running toward her room, hiding herself under the covers next to her mother.

I ran too. I've been running all my life. Because every night, a woman in a thick, grey, knitted jumper walks the hospital's corridors. She carries a folder. She has all our names written inside.

It's Christmas Eve, and by the time you wake up the snow will probably have melted. Snow never lasts very long in Helsingborg. It's the only place I know where the wind comes at an angle from below, like it's frisking you. Where the umbrellas protect you better if you hold them upside down. I was born here but I've never gotten used to it; Helsingborg and I will never find peace. Maybe everyone feels that way about their hometown: the place we're from never apologizes, never admits that it was wrong about us. It just sits there, at the end of the motorway, whispering: "You might be all rich and powerful now. And maybe you do come home with expensive watches and fancy clothes. But you can't fool me, because I know who you really are. You're just a scared little boy."

I met death by the side of my wrecked car last

night, after the accident. My blood was everywhere. The woman in the grey jumper was standing next to me with a disapproving look on her face and she said: "You shouldn't be here." I was so scared of her, because I'm a winner, a survivor. And all survivors are scared of death. That's why we're still here. My face was cut to shreds, my shoulder out of joint, and I was trapped inside 1.5 million kronors' worth of steel and technology.

When I saw the woman, I shouted, "Take someone else! I can give you someone else to kill!"

But she just leaned forward, looked disappointed, and said: "It doesn't work like that. I don't make the decisions. I just look after the logistics and the transportation."

"For who? For God or the Devil, or . . . someone else?" I sobbed.

She sighed. "I stay out of the politics. I just do my job. Now give me my folder."

It wasn't the car crash that brought me to the hospital, I was there long before that. Cancer. I'd met the girl for the first time six days earlier, when I was smoking on the fire escape so the nurses wouldn't see me. They went on and on about smoking, as though it would have time to kill me.

The door to the corridor was ajar, and I could hear the girl talking to her mother in the TV room. They played the same game every night; when the hospital was so quiet that you could hear the snowflakes bouncing against the windows like good-night kisses, the mother whispered to the girl: "What are you going to be when you grow up?"

The girl knew the game was for her mother's sake, but she pretended it was for hers. She laughed as she said, "doctor" and "engineeeer," plus her perennial favorite: "space hunter."

Once the mother fell asleep in an armchair, the girl stayed where she was, coloring in the chair which wanted to be red and talking to Babbit whose name was that. "Is it cold on death?" she asked Babbit. But Babbit didn't know. So the girl packed thick gloves in her backpack, just to be on the safe side.

She spotted me through the glass. She wasn't scared, I remember being furious at her parents for that. What kind of adult doesn't raise their kid to be terrified of a strange, forty-five-year-old, chain-smoking bloke who's staring at her from a fire escape? But this girl wasn't scared. She waved. I waved back. She grabbed Babbit's paw, came over to the door and spoke through the crack.

"Do you have cancer too?"

"Yes," I replied. Because that was the truth.

"Are you famous? You're in a picture in Mummy's newspaper."

"Yes," I replied. Because that was also the truth. The papers wrote about my money, no one knew I was ill yet, but I'm the kind of person whose diagnosis will make the news. I'm not an ordinary person, everyone will hear about it when I die. When five-year-old girls die, no one writes about that, there aren't any memorials in the evening papers, their feet are still too small, they haven't had time to make anyone care about their footsteps yet. But people care about me because of what I'll leave behind, what I've built and achieved, businesses and properties and assets. Money isn't money to me, not like it is to you. I save and calculate and don't worry about it. It's nothing but points for me, just a measure of my success.

"It's not the same cancer you have," I said to the girl. Because that was my only consolation in the diagnosis. That the doctor had apologetically explained: "You have a very, very unusual type of cancer."

I don't even get cancer like you people.

The girl blinked firmly and asked: "Is it cold on death?"

"I don't know," I said.

I should have said something else. Something bigger. But I'm not that man. So I just dropped my cigarette and mumbled: "You should stop drawing on the furniture."

I know what you're thinking: what a bastard I am. And you're right. But the vast majority of successful people don't become bastards, we were bastards long before. That's why we've been successful.

"You're allowed to draw on the furniture when you have cancer," the girl suddenly exclaimed with a shrug. "No one says anything."

I don't know what it was about that, but I started to laugh. When had I last done that? She laughed too. Then she and Babbit ran off to their room.

t's so easy to kill someone, all a person like me needs is a car and a few seconds. Because people like you trust me, you drive thousands of kilos of metal at hundreds of kilometers an hour, hurtling through the darkness with the people you love most sleeping in the backseat, and when someone like me approaches from the opposite direction, you trust that I don't have bad brakes. That I'm not looking for my phone between the seats, not driving too fast, not drifting between lanes because I'm blinking the tears from my eyes. That I'm not sitting on the slip road to the 111 with my headlights out, just waiting for a lorry. You trust me. That I'm not drunk. That I'm not going to kill you.

The woman with the grey sweater pulled me out of the wreckage this morning. She wiped my blood from her folder.

"Kill someone . . . else," I begged.

She took a resigned breath through her nose.

"It doesn't work like that. I don't have that kind of influence. I can't just swap a death for a death. I have to swap a life for a life."

"Do it, then!" I screamed.

The woman shook her head sadly, reached out and pulled a cigarette from my breast pocket. It was bent, but not broken. She smoked it in two long drags.

"I've actually given up," she said defensively.

I lay bleeding on the ground and pointed to the folder.

"Is my name in there?"

"Everyone's is."

"What do you mean, *a life for a life*?"

She groaned.

"You really are an idiot. You always have been."

At one point in time, you were mine. My son.

The girl at the hospital reminded me of you. Something happened when you were born. You cried so loudly, and it was the first time it had happened to me: the first time I'd felt pain for someone else. I couldn't stay with someone who had that kind of power over me.

Every parent will take five minutes in the car outside the house from time to time, just sitting there. Just breathing and gathering the strength to head back inside to all of their responsibilities. The suffocating expectation of being good, coping. Every parent will take ten seconds in the stairwell occasionally, key in hand, not putting it in the lock. I was honest, I only waited a moment before I ran. I spent your entire childhood travelling. You were the girl's age when you asked what I did. I told you I made money. You said everyone did that. I said, "No, the majority of people just survive, they think their things have a value but nothing does. Things only have a price, based on expectation, and I do business with that. The only thing of value on Earth is time. One second will always be a second, there's no negotiating with that."

You despise me now, because I've devoted all my seconds to my work. But I have, at least, devoted them to something. What have your friends' parents devoted their lives to? Barbecues and rounds of golf? Charter holidays and TV shows? What will they leave behind?

You hate me now, but you were once mine. You once sat on my lap and were terrified of the starry sky. Someone had told you that the stars aren't really above us but below, and that the earth spun so quickly that if you were small and light you could easily fall off, straight into all that darkness. The porch door was open, your mother was listening to Leonard Cohen, so I told you that we actually lived deep in a cozy grotto and that the sky was like a stone covering the opening. "Then what are the stars?" you asked, and I told you they were cracks, through which the light could trickle in. Then I said that your eyes were the same thing, to me. Tiny, tiny cracks, through which the light could trickle out. You laughed so loudly then. Have you ever laughed like that since? I laughed too. I, who had wanted to live a life high above everyone else, ended up with a son who would rather live deep beneath the surface.

In the living room, your mother turned up the volume and danced, laughing, on the other side of the window. You crawled higher in my lap. We were a family then, albeit fleetingly. I belonged to you both, for a moment or two.

I know you wished you had an ordinary father. One who didn't travel, wasn't famous, one who would have been happy with just two eyes on him: yours. You never wanted to say your surname and hear, "Sorry, but is your dad . . . ?" But I was too important for that. I didn't take

you to school, didn't hold your hand, didn't help you blow out your birthday candles, I never fell asleep in your bed, halfway through our fourth bedtime story, with your cheek on my collarbone. But you'll have everything that everyone else longs for: Wealth. Freedom. I abandoned you, but at least I abandoned you at the top of the hierarchy of needs.

But you don't care about that, do you? You're your mother's son. She was smarter than me, I never quite forgave her for that. She also felt more than me, that was her weakness, and it meant I could hurt her with words. You might not remember when she left me, you were still so small, but the truth is that I didn't even notice. I came home after a trip and it took me two days to realize that neither of you was there.

Several years later, when you were eleven or twelve, the two of you had a huge argument about something and you took a bus to my house in the middle of the night and said you wanted to live with me. I said no. You were completely beside yourself, sobbing and crying on the rug in my hallway, screaming that it wasn't fair.

I looked you in the eye and said: "Life isn't fair."

You bit your lip. Lowered your eyes and replied: "Lucky for you."

You might have stopped being mine that day, I don't know. Maybe that's when I lost you. If that's the case, I was wrong. If that's the case, life is fair.

our nights ago, the girl knocked on the window again.

"Do you want to play?" she asked.

"What?" I said.

"I'm bored. Do you want to play?"

I told her she should go to bed. Because I'm the person you think I am, the kind of person who says no when a dying five-year-old wants to play. She and Babbit went off towards her room, but the girl turned around and looked at me and asked: "Are you brave too?"

"What?"

"Everyone always says I'm so brave."

Her eyelids fluttered. So I replied honestly: "Don't be brave. If you're scared, be scared. All survivors are."

"Are you? Of the woman with the folder?"

I took a calm drag on my cigarette, nodded slowly.

"Me too," said the girl.

She and Babbit walked towards her room. I don't know what happened then. Maybe I cracked, making all the light spill out. Or in. I'm not evil, even I understand that cancer should have an age limit. So I opened my mouth and said: "Not tonight. I'll stay here and keep watch, so she doesn't come tonight."

The girl smiled then.

The next morning, I was sitting awake on the floor in the corridor. I heard the girl and her mother playing a new game. The mother asked, "Who do you want to invite to your next birthday party?" even though there wouldn't be a next one. And the girl played along, reeled off the names of everyone she loved. It's a long list when you're five. That morning, I was on it.

'm an egoist, you learnt that early on. Your mother once screamed that I'm the kind of person who doesn't have any equals, I only have people above me that I want something from and people beneath me who I trample on. She was right, so I kept going until there was no one left above me.

But just how big is my egoism? You know that I can buy and sell everything, but would I clamber over dead bodies? Would I kill someone?

I had a brother. I've never told you that. He was dead when we were born. Maybe there was only room for one of us on this earth, and I wanted it more. I clambered over my brother in the womb. I was a winner, even then.

The woman with the folder was there, at the hospital. I've seen the pictures. Sometimes, when my mother drank alone at night, she fell asleep too drunk to remember to hide them. The woman was everywhere in those photos, an out of focus figure outside windows, a blur in the corridors. In one from the day before our birth, she was standing in the queue behind my parents at a petrol station. Mum was heavily pregnant. Dad was laughing in that picture. I never saw him do that. Throughout my life, he only ever smiled.

When I was five, I saw the woman with the folder by some train tracks. I was about to cross when she leapt forward from the other side and shouted something. I stopped dead, astonished. The train appeared a second later, thundering by so close that I fell over. By the time it had passed, she was gone.

When I was fifteen, my best friend and I were playing on the rocks by the sea in Kullaberg and halfway up we passed a woman in a grey sweater. "Be careful, these rocks are treacherous when it rains," she mumbled. I didn't recognize her until she was already gone.

It started raining half an hour later, and my best friend fell headlong. The rain was still falling during his funeral, as though it never planned to stop. I saw the woman as I was leaving the church, she was standing beneath an umbrella in the square, but the rain was still flecking her cheeks, the way it only does in Helsingborg.

When my dad got sick, I saw her outside his room in the care home, on his last night. I came out of the toilet, she didn't notice me. She was wearing the same grey sweater, writing something in her folder with a black pencil. Then she went into his room and never came out again. Dad was dead the next morning.

When my mum got sick, I was working abroad. We spoke on the phone, she was so weak when she whispered: "The doctor says everything looks normal." So that I wouldn't worry about her dying a dramatic death. My parents always wanted everything to be like normal. Ever since my brother died, they just wanted to be like everyone else. Maybe that's why I became exceptional, out of sheer obstinacy. Mum passed away during the night, I hired an appraiser to go through her flat and her possessions; he sent me photos. In one of them, from the bedroom, there was a black pencil on the floor. By the time I got home, it was gone. Mum's slippers were in the hallway, and there were small clumps of grey wool on their soles.

failed with you. Fathers are meant to teach their sons about life, but you were a disappointment.

You called me on my birthday last autumn, I was forty-five. You had just turned twenty. You told me that you'd got a job in the old Tivoli building. The city had moved the entire building right across the square to make room for new private flats. You said the word "private" with such disgust, because we're so different. You see history, I see development, you see nostalgia, I see weakness. I could have given you a job, could have given you hundreds of jobs, but you wanted to be a bartender at Vinylbaren, in a building that had been ready to fall down even when it was a steamboat station four generations earlier. I bluntly asked you whether you were happy. Because I am who I am. And you replied: "It's good enough,

Dad. Good enough." Because you knew I hated that phrase. You were always someone who could be happy. You don't know how much of a blessing that is.

Maybe it was your mother who forced you to call; I think she suspected I was sick, but you invited me down to the bar. You said they served *smørrebrød* in the café; you remembered that I always used to eat it when you and I took the ferry to Denmark at Christmas when you were small. Your mother had nagged me to do something special with you, at least once a year, I think you know that. But I couldn't sit still and talk, I needed to be on the way somewhere, and you got travel sick in the car. So we liked the ferry, both of us, me the way there and you the way back. I loved leaving everything behind, but you loved standing out on deck and watching Helsingborg appear on the horizon. The way home, the silhouette of something you recognized. You loved it.

I sat in my car in Hamntorget last autumn, saw you

through the window of the bar. You were making cocktails and making people laugh. I didn't go in, I was afraid I would end up telling you that I had cancer. I wouldn't have been able to deal with your compassion. And I was drunk, of course, so I remembered the steps outside the house where you and your mother lived, and all the times you had sat there waiting for me when I didn't turn up like I'd promised. All the occasions I'd wasted your time. I remembered the ferries at Christmas, always early in the morning so that we would get home in time for me to spend the rest of the day drinking. Our last trip was when you were fourteen, I taught you to play poker in a basement bar in Helsingør, showed you how to identify the losers at a table: weak men with strong schnapps. I taught you to capitalize on those who couldn't understand the game. You won six hundred kronor. I wanted to keep playing, but you gave me a pleading look and said, "Six hundred's good enough, Dad."

You stopped at a jewelry shop on the way back to the ferry and bought some earrings with the money. It took me a whole year to realize that they weren't for some girl you were trying to charm. They were for your mother.

You never played poker again.

I failed with you. I tried to make you tough. You ended up kind.

Late last night, at the hospital, the woman with the folder came walking down the corridor. She stopped when she saw me. I didn't run. I remembered all the times I had seen her before. When she took my brother away. When she took my best friend. When she took my parents. I wasn't going to be scared anymore, I'd keep that power at least, down to the last moment.

"I know who you are," I said, without a single tremor in my voice. "You're death."

The woman frowned and looked deeply, deeply offended. "I'm not death," she muttered. "I'm *not* my job."

That knocked the air out of me. I'll admit it. It's not what you expect to hear at a moment like that.

The woman's eyebrows lowered as she repeated: "I'm not death. I just do the picking up and dropping off."

45

"I—" I began, but she interrupted me.

"You're so self-obsessed that you think I've been chasing you all your life. But I've been looking out for you. Of all the idiots I could have picked as my favorite . . ." She massaged her temples.

"Fa . . . favorite?" I stuttered.

She reached out and touched my shoulder. Her fingers were cold, they moved down towards my breast pocket and took a cigarette. She lit it, clutched her folder tight. Maybe it was just the smoke, but a lonely tear ran down her cheek as she whispered: "It's against the rules for us to have favorites. It makes us dangerous, if we do. But sometimes . . . sometimes we have bad days at work too. You screamed so loudly when I came to get your brother, and I turned around and happened to look you in the eye. We're not meant to do that."

My voice broke when I asked: "Did you know . . . everything I've become, everything I've achieved . . . did you know? Was that why you took my brother instead of me?" She shook her head. "It doesn't work like that. We don't know the future, we just do our job. But I made a mistake with you. I looked you in the eye and it . . . hurt. We're not meant to hurt."

"Did I kill my brother?" I sniffed.

"No," she said.

I sobbed despairingly. "Then why did you take him? Why do you take everyone I love?"

She gently placed her hand in my hair. Whispered: "It's not down to us who goes and who stays. That's why it's against the rules for us to hurt."

When the doctor gave me the diagnosis, I didn't have an awakening, I just did my accounts. Everything I'd built, the footprints I've left behind. Weak people always look at people like me and say, "He's rich, but is he *happy*?" As though that was a relevant measure of anything. Happiness is for children and animals, it doesn't have any biological function. Happy people don't create anything, their world is one without art and music and skyscrapers, without discoveries and innovations. All leaders, all of your heroes, they've been obsessed. Happy people don't get obsessed, they don't devote their lives to curing illnesses or making planes take off. The happy leave nothing behind. They live for the sake of living, they're only on earth as consumers. Not me.

But something happened. I walked along the beach

out by Råå, the morning after the diagnosis, and I saw two dogs running into the sea, playing in the waves. And I wondered: Have you ever been like that, as happy as they are? Could you be that happy? Would it be worth it?

The woman lifted her hand from my hair. She seemed almost ashamed.

"We're not meant to feel things. But I'm not . . . just my job. I have . . . interests too. I knit."

She gestured to her grey sweater. I tried to nod appreciatively, because it felt like she expected it. She nodded back with smoke in her eyes. I took the deepest breath of my life.

"I know you're here to collect me now. And I'm ready to die," I managed. As though it were a prayer. And then she said the one thing I feared even more: "I'm not here for you. Not yet. You'll find out tomorrow that you're healthy. You'll live for a long while yet, you'll have time to achieve whatever you want."

I trembled. Hugged myself like a child and sobbed. "Then what are you doing here?"

"My job."

She patted me gently on the cheek. Then she walked off down the corridor, stopped outside a door and opened her folder. Slowly pulled out a black pencil and crossed out a name. Then she opened the door to the girl's room.

The day before yesterday, I heard the girl and her mother arguing. The girl wanted to make a milk-carton dinosaur, but there wasn't time. The girl got angry, the mother cried. The girl stopped then, the corners of her mouth jumping over the despair leaving her eyes as though it was a skipping rope, and she held her mother's hand and said: "Okay, then. But what about a game?"

They had one where they pretended to talk on the phone. The mother said she had been taken captive by pirates, that she was on her way to their secret island to help the pirates build a flying pirate ship, and in exchange they would sail her home again. The girl laughed and forced her mother to promise that they would build a milk-carton dinosaur *then*! After that, the girl explained that she was on a space ship with "alianies." "Aliens," her mother corrected her. "Alianies," the girl corrected. "They've got mysterious machines with huge buttons and they stick wires into my arms and they have masks over their faces and uniforms that rustle and you can only see their heads. And they whisper, 'There there, there there, there there,' and then they count down from ten. And when they get to one you go to sleep. Even though you try not to!"

The girl fell silent, because the mother was crying then, even though it was just a game. So the girl whispered: "The alianies will save me, Mummy. They're the best."

The mother tried not to kiss her a million times. The nurses came and lifted the girl onto the rolling bed to take her to the operating theater. They passed mysterious machines with huge buttons. The girl had wires stuck to her arms and the alianies wore uniforms which rustled and masks over their faces and when they leaned over the edge of the bed all she could see was their heads. They whispered, "There there, there there, there there," and then counted down from ten. And when they got to one, the girl fell asleep. Even though she tried not to.

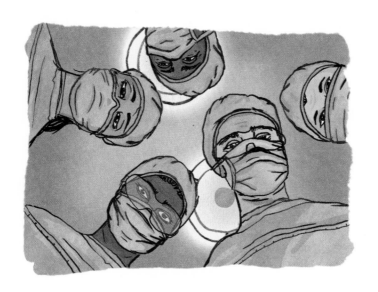

t's bloody awful to admit to yourself that you're not the kind of person you've always thought you were. All you normal people would have tried to save the child if you could, wouldn't you? Of course you would. So when the woman with the grey sweater opened the door to the girl's room, part of me cracked, because it turns out that I'm more normal than I thought. I shoved the woman, grabbed the folder, and then I ran. As though I were one of you.

My car was parked outside the hospital; the brake lights never came on. The wheels grappled for something to cling onto in the snow. I drove down Bergaliden toward town, and then took Strandvägen north, toward the sea. The most beautiful stretch in the world. I thundered between the trees by Sofiero Castle, towards the terraced houses in Laröd, and didn't slow down before I reached the 111. There, on the slip road to the bigger road, I stopped and turned off the headlights. As the lorry approached, I drove straight out. I don't remember the crash, just the pain in my ears and the light which washed over me as the steel crumpled like foil. And the blood, everywhere.

The woman dragged both me and the folder out of the wreck. When I shouted, "I can give you someone else to kill!" she realized that I meant myself. But it made no difference. She couldn't take a death for a death. Only a life for a life.

I lay there on the ground with all of Helsingborg's winds beneath my clothes, and she patiently explained: "It's not enough for you to die. To make room for the girl's entire life, another life has to cease to exist. I have to delete its contents. So if you give your life, it'll disappear. You won't die, you'll never have existed. No one will remember you. You were never here."

A life for a life. That's what it means.

That was why she brought me to you. She had to show me what I was giving up.

An hour ago, we were standing in Hamntorget watching you clean the bar through the window. "You never get your child's attention back," your mother once said. "The time when they don't just listen to you to be nice, that time passes, it's the first thing to go."

The woman stood beside me and pointed at you. "If you give your life for the girl at the hospital, you'll never have been his."

I blinked, out of step.

"If I die . . ."

"You won't die," she corrected me. "You'll be erased."

"But . . . if I don't . . . If I've never . . ."

She wearily shook her head at my lack of understanding. "Your son will still exist, but he'll have a different father. Everything you'll leave behind will still exist, but it'll have been built by someone else. Your footprints will vanish, you'll never have existed. You humans always think you're ready to give your lives, but only until you understand what that really involves. You're obsessed with your legacy, aren't you? You can't bear to die and be forgotten."

I didn't answer for quite some time. I thought about whether you would have done it, given your life for someone else. You probably would. Because you're your mother's son, and she's already given a life. The one she could have lived if she hadn't lived for you and for me.

I turned to the woman. "I've sat here watching him every evening since I got sick."

She nodded. "I know."

I knew that she knew. I'd understood that much by now. "Every night, I wondered whether it was possible to change a person."

"What did you conclude?"

"That we are who we are."

She started walking straight toward you then. I panicked. "Where are you going?" I shouted.

"I need to be sure that you're sure," she replied, crossing the car park and knocking on the door of Vinylbaren.

I ran after her and hissed: "Can he see us?"

I don't know what I was expecting. The woman turned to me, mockingly raised one eyebrow and replied: "I'm not a bloody ghost. Of course he can see us!"

When you opened the door, she muttered, "I need a beer," without paying any attention as you patiently—like your mother would have done—tried to explain that unfortunately the bar was closed. Then you saw me. I think both of our worlds probably came to a standstill right then.

You didn't say anything about my ripped suit, or the blood on my face, you'd seen me in a worse state before. The woman in the grey sweater ate smørrebrød and drank three beers in a row, but I asked for a coffee. I saw how happy that made you. We said very little, because there was too much I wanted to say. That's always when we fall silent. You wiped the bar and sorted the glasses, and I thought about the love in your hands. You've always touched the things you like as though they had a pulse. You cared about that bar, adored this town. The people and the buildings and the night as it approached over the Sound. Even the wind and the useless soccer team. This has always been your town in a way it never was for me; you never tried to find a life, you were in the right place from the start.

I told the woman in the grey sweater what you had told me: that they had moved the entire Tivoli building right across the square. That's what fathers do, they sit in front of their sons and tell their son's stories to a third person rather than letting them speak for themselves. The woman looked at me for intervals which were far too short between blinks.

"You don't care?" I asked.

"I really, really, really don't," she replied.

And you laughed then. Loudly. It made me sing inside.

I asked questions, you answered. You told me that you had designed everything in the bar with respect for the building's history. It showed. I should have told you that. Not for your sake, because you won't remember any of this, but for mine. I should have told you I was proud.

You cleared everything away and I followed you, awkwardly, clutching my coffee cup. You turned around to take it, and our hands briefly overlapped. I felt your heart beat, right in the ends of your fingertips.

You glanced at the woman in the bar, she was reading the cocktail menu and had paused on one containing "gin, lime, pastis, and triple sec." Its name was *Corpse Reviver No. 3.* She laughed at that, and then you laughed too, though you found it funny for completely different reasons.

"I'm glad you've met someone who's . . . you know . . . your own age," you said quietly to me.

I didn't know what to reply. So I didn't.

You smiled and kissed me on the cheek. "Merry Christmas, Dad."

My heart fell to the floor and you walked through the door into the kitchen. I couldn't bring myself to let you come back. A second is always a second; that's the one definitive value we have on earth. Everyone is always negotiating, all of the time. You're doing the deal of your life, every day. This was mine.

The woman drank the last of her beer. Picked up the folder from the bar. We went to the outdoor seating area; there's fierce competition for the most beautiful view in Helsingborg, but that particular place is so calm and confident. It doesn't need to show off, it knows its own beauty. The waves rolling in, the ferries anchored in the harbor, Denmark waiting on the other side of the water.

"How does this work?" I asked.

"We jump inwards," the woman replied.

"Does it hurt?" I asked.

She nodded sadly.

"I'm scared," I admitted, but she shook her head.

"You're not scared. You're just grieving. No one tells you humans that your sorrow feels like fear."

"What are we grieving?"

"Time."

I nodded toward the windows in the bar and whispered: "Will he remember anything?"

She shook her head. "Sometimes, for a second, he might feel like there's something missing. But . . . then . . ." She clicked her fingers.

"And the girl?"

"She'll live her life."

"Will you keep watch over them?"

The woman nodded slowly. "I've never liked the rules anyway."

I buttoned my jacket. The wind was blowing at an angle from below. "Is it cold . . . where we're going?" I asked.

But the woman didn't reply. She just handed me a pair of knitted gloves. They were grey, but there was a single thin red thread hanging from one of them. She pulled a small pair of scissors from one of her pockets and carefully cut it away. Then she held my hands as we jumped inwards. You'll never read this. You've never sat waiting on the steps outside your mother's house. I've never wasted your time.

And as we jumped inwards, the woman with the folder and I, I saw Helsingborg as you've always seen it, for the briefest of moments. Like the silhouette of something you recognize. A home. It was our town then, finally, yours and mine.

And that was good enough.

You'll wake up soon. It's Christmas Eve morning. And I loved you.

AND
EVERY MORNING
THE WAY HOME GETS
LONGER AND LONGER

a novella

Dear Reader,

One of my idols once said, "The worst part about grow-ing old is that I don't get any ideas anymore." Those words have never quite left me since I first heard them, because this would be my greatest fear: imagination giving up before the body does. I guess I'm not alone in this. Humans are a strange breed in the way our fear of getting old seems to be even greater than our fear of dying.

This is a story about memories and about letting go. It's a love letter and a slow farewell between a man and his grandson, and between a dad and his boy.

I never meant for you to read it, to be quite hon-est. I wrote it just because I was trying to sort out my own thoughts, and I'm the kind of person who needs to see what I'm thinking on paper to make sense of it. But it turned into a small tale of how I'm dealing with slowly losing the greatest minds I know, about missing someone who is still here, and how I wanted to explain it all to my children. I'm letting it go now, for what it's worth.

It's about fear and love, and how they seem to go hand in hand most of the time. Most of all, it's about time. While we still have it. Thank you for giving this story yours.

Fredrik Backman

There's a hospital room at the end of a life where someone, right in the middle of the floor, has pitched a green tent. A person wakes up inside it, breathless and afraid, not knowing where he is. A young man sitting next to him whispers:

"Don't be scared."

Isn't that the best of all life's ages, an old man thinks as he looks at his grandchild. When a boy is just big enough to know how the world works but still young enough to refuse to accept it. Noah's feet don't touch the ground when his legs dangle over the edge of the bench, but his head reaches all the way to space, because he hasn't been alive long enough to allow anyone to keep his thoughts on Earth. His grandpa is next to him and is incredibly old, of course, so old now that people have given up and no longer nag him to start acting like an adult. So old that it's too late to grow up. It's not so bad either, that age.

The bench is in a square; Noah blinks heavily at the sunrise beyond it, newly woken. He doesn't want to admit to Grandpa that he doesn't know where they are, because this has always been their game: Noah closes his eyes and Grandpa takes him somewhere they've never been before. Sometimes the boy has to squeeze his eyes tight, tight shut while he and Grandpa change buses four times in town, and sometimes Grandpa just takes him straight into the woods behind the house by the lake. Sometimes they go in the boat, often for so long that Noah falls asleep, and once they've made it far enough Grandpa whispers "open your eyes" and gives Noah a map and a compass and the task of working out how they're going to get home. Grandpa knows he'll always manage, because there are two things in life in which Grandpa's faith is unwavering: mathematics and his grandson. A group of people calculated how to fly three men to the moon when Grandpa was young, and mathematics took them all the way there and back again. Numbers always lead people back.

But this place lacks coordinates; there are no roads out, no maps lead here.

Noah remembers that Grandpa asked him to close his eyes today. He remembers that they crept out of Grandpa's house and he knows that Grandpa took him to the lake, because the boy knows all the sounds and songs of the water, eyes open or not. He remembers damp wood underfoot as they stepped into the boat, but nothing after that. He doesn't know how he and Grandpa ended up here, on a bench in a round square. The place is strange but everything here is familiar, like someone stole all the things you grew up with and put them into the wrong house. There's a desk over there, just like the one in Grandpa's office, with a mini calculator and squared notepaper on top. Grandpa whistles gently, a sad tune, takes a quick little break to whisper:

"The square got smaller overnight again."

Then he starts whistling again. Grandpa seems surprised when the boy gives him a questioning look, aware for the first time that he said those words aloud.

"Sorry, Noahnoah, I forgot that thoughts aren't silent here."

Grandpa always calls him "Noahnoah" because he likes his grandson's name twice as much as everyone else's. He puts a hand in the boy's hair, not ruffling it, just letting his fingers rest there.

"There's nothing to be afraid of, Noahnoah."

Hyacinths are blooming beneath the bench, a million tiny purple arms reaching up from the stalks to embrace the rays of sunlight. The boy recognizes the flowers, they're Grandma's, they smell like Christmas. For other children maybe that scent would be ginger biscuits and mulled wine, but if you've ever had a Grandma who loved things that grew then Christmas will always smell like hyacinths. There are shards of glass and keys glittering between the flowers, like

someone had been keeping them safe in a big jar but then fell over and dropped it.

"What are all those keys for?" the boy asks.

"Which keys?" asks Grandpa.

The old man's eyes are strangely empty now. He raps his temples in frustration. The boy opens his mouth to say something, but stops himself when he sees that. He sits quietly instead and does what Grandpa taught him to do if he gets lost: take in his surroundings, look for landmarks and clues. The bench is surrounded by trees, because Grandpa loves trees, because trees don't give a damn what people think. Silhouettes of birds lift up from them, spread out across the heavens, and rest confidently on the winds. A dragon is crossing the square, green and sleepy, and a penguin with small chocolate-colored handprints on its stomach is sleeping in one corner. A soft owl with only one eye is sitting next to it. Noah recognizes them too; they used to be his. Grandpa gave him the dragon when he had just been born, be-

cause Grandma said it wasn't suitable to give newborn children dragons as cuddly toys and Grandpa said he didn't want a suitable grandson.

People are walking around the square, but they're blurry. When the boy tries to focus on their outlines they slip from his eyes like light through venetian blinds. One of them stops and waves to Grandpa. Grandpa waves back, tries to look confident.

"Who's that?" the boy asks.

"That's . . . I . . . I can't remember, Noahnoah. It was so long ago . . . I think . . ."

He falls silent, hesitates, and searches for something in his pockets.

"You haven't given me a map and a compass today, nothing to count on, I don't know how I'm meant to find the way home, Grandpa," Noah whispers.

"I'm afraid those things won't help us here, Noah-noah."

"Where are we, Grandpa?"

Then Grandpa starts to cry, silently and tearlessly, so that his grandson won't realize.

"It's hard to explain, Noahnoah. It's so incredibly, incredibly hard to explain."

The girl is standing in front of him and smells like hyacinths, like she's never been anywhere else. Her hair is old but the wind in it is new, and he still remembers what it felt like to fall in love; that's the last memory to abandon him. Falling in love with her meant having no room in his own body. That was why he danced.

"We had too little time," he says.

She shakes her head.

"We had an eternity. Children and grandchildren."

"I only had you for the blink of an eye," he says.

She laughs.

"You had me an entire lifetime. All of mine."

"That wasn't enough."

She kisses his wrist; her chin rests in his fingers.

"No."

They walk slowly along a road he thinks he has walked before, not remembering where it leads. His hand is wrapped safely around hers and they're sixteen again, no shaking fingers, no aching hearts. His chest tells him he could run to the horizon, but one breath passes and his lungs won't obey him anymore. She stops, waits patiently beneath the weight of his arm, and she's old now, like the day before she left him. He whispers into her eyelid:

"I don't know how to explain it to Noah."

"I know," she says and her breath sings against his neck.

"He's so big now, I wish you could see him."

"I do, I do."

"I miss you, my love."

"I'm still with you, darling difficult you."

"But only in my memories now. Only here."

"That doesn't matter. This was always my favorite part of you."

"I've filled the square. It got smaller overnight again."

"I know, I know."

Then she dabs his forehead with a soft handkerchief, making small red circles bloom on the material, and she admonishes him:

"You're bleeding; you need to be careful when you get into the boat."

He closes his eyes.

"What do I say to Noah? How do I explain that I'm going to be leaving him even before I die?"

She takes his jaw in her hands and kisses him.

"Darling difficult husband, you should explain this to our grandson the way you've always explained everything to him: as though he was smarter than you."

He holds her close. He knows the rain will be coming soon.

Noah can see that Grandpa is ashamed the minute he says it's hard to explain, because Grandpa never says that to Noah. All other adults do, Noah's dad does it every day, but not Grandpa.

"I don't mean it would be hard for you to understand, Noahnoah. I mean it's hard for me to understand," the old man apologizes.

"You're bleeding!" the boy cries.

Grandpa's fingers fumble across his forehead. A single drop of blood is teetering on the edge of a deep gash in his skin, right above his eyebrow, sitting there fighting gravity. Eventually it falls, onto Grandpa's shirt, and two more drops immediately do the same, just like when children leap into the sea from a jetty, one has to be brave enough to go first before the others will follow.

"Yes . . . yes, I suppose I am, I must've . . . fallen," Grandpa broods as though that should have been a thought too.

But there are no silent thoughts here. The boy's eyes widen.

"Wait, you . . . you fell in the boat. I remember now! That's how you hurt yourself, I shouted for Dad!"

"Dad?" Grandpa repeats.

"Yeah, don't be scared, Grandpa, Dad's coming to get us soon!" Noah promises as he pats Grandpa on the forearm, soothing him with a degree of experience far beyond what a boy his age should have.

Grandpa's pupils bounce anxiously, so the boy resolutely continues:

"Do you remember what you always said when we went fishing on the island and slept in the tent? There's nothing wrong with being a bit scared, you said, because if you wet yourself it'll keep the bears away!"

Grandpa blinks tightly, as though even Noah's outline has gotten blurry, but then the old man nods several times, his eyes clearer.

"Yes! Yes, so I did, Noahnoah, I said that, didn't I? When we were fishing. Oh, darling Noahnoah, you've grown so big. So very big. How is school?"

Noah steadies his voice, tries to swallow the trembling of his vocal cords as his heart pounds in alarm.

"It's fine. I'm top of the class in math. Just keep calm, Grandpa; Dad's going to come and get us soon."

Grandpa's hand rests on the boy's shoulder.

"That's good, Noahnoah, that's good. Mathematics will always lead you home."

The boy is terrified now, but knows better than to let Grandpa see that, so he shouts:

"Three point one four one!"

"Five nine two," Grandpa immediately replies.

"Six five three," the boy reels off.

"Five eight nine." Grandpa laughs.

That's another of Grandpa's favorite games, reciting the decimals of pi, the mathematical constant which is the key to calculating the size of a circle. Grandpa loves the magic of it, those key numbers which unlock secrets, open up the entire universe to us. He knows more than two hundred decimals of it by heart; the boy's record is half that. Grandpa always says that the years will allow them to meet in the middle, when the boy's thoughts expand and Grandpa's contract.

"Seven," says the boy.

"Nine," Grandpa whispers.

The boy squeezes his rough palm, and Grandpa sees that he is afraid, so the old man says:

"Have I ever told you about the time I went to the doctor, Noahnoah? I said, 'Doctor, Doctor, I've broken my arm in two places!' and the doctor replied, 'Then I'd advise you to stop going there!'"

The boy blinks; things are becoming increasingly blurred.

"You've told that one before, Grandpa. It's your favorite joke."

"Oh," Grandpa whispers, ashamed.

The square is a perfect circle. The wind fights in the treetops; the leaves move in a hundred dialects of green; Grandpa has always loved this time of year. Warm winds wander through the arms of the hyacinths and small drops of blood dry on his forehead. Noah holds his fingers there and asks:

"Where are we, Grandpa? Why are my stuffed animals here in the square? What happened when you fell in the boat?"

And then Grandpa's tears leave his eyelashes.

"We're in my brain, Noahnoah. And it got smaller overnight again."

Ted and his dad are in a garden. It smells like hyacinths.

"How is school?" the dad asks gruffly.

He always asks that and Ted can never give the right answer. The dad likes numbers and the boy likes letters; they're different languages.

"I got top marks for my essay," says the boy.

"And mathematics? How are you doing in mathematics? How are words meant to guide you home if you're lost in the woods?" the dad grunts.

The boy doesn't reply; he doesn't understand numbers, or maybe the numbers don't understand him. They've never seen eye to eye, his dad and him.

The dad, still a young man, bends down and starts pulling weeds from a flower bed. When he gets back up it's dark, though he could swear only a moment had passed.

"Three point one four one," he mumbles, but the voice no longer sounds like his own.

"Dad?" says the son's voice, but different now, deeper.

"Three point one four one! It's your favorite game!" roars the dad.

"No," the son softly replies.

"It was your . . ." the dad starts, but the air betrays his words.

"You're bleeding, Dad," says the boy.

The dad blinks at him several times, but then shakes his head and chuckles exaggeratedly.

"Ah, it's just a graze. Have I ever told you about the time I went to the doctor? I said, 'Doctor, Doctor, I've broken my arm. . . .' "

He falls silent.

"You're bleeding, Dad," the boy repeats patiently.

"I said, 'I've broken my arm.' Or no, wait, I said . . . I can't remember . . . it's my favorite joke, Ted. It's my favorite joke. Stop pulling at me, I can tell my favorite bloody joke!"

The boy carefully takes hold of his hands, but they're small now.

The boy's are like spades in comparison.

"Whose hands are these?" the old man pants.

"They're mine," Ted replies.

The dad shakes his head; blood runs from his forehead, anger fills his eyes.

"Where's my boy? Where's my little boy? Answer me!"

"Sit down a minute, Dad," Ted begs.

The dad's pupils hunt the dusk around the treetops; he tries to cry out but can't remember how; his throat will only give him hissing sounds now.

"How is school, Ted? How are you doing in mathematics?"

Mathematics will always lead you home. . . .

"You need to sit down, Dad, you're bleeding," the son begs.

He has a beard; it bristles beneath the dad's palm when he touches the boy's cheek.

"What happened?" whispers the dad.

"You fell over in the boat. I told you not to go out in

the boat, Dad. It's dangerous, especially when you take No—"

The dad's eyes widen and he excitedly interrupts:

"Ted? Is that you? You've changed! How is school?"

Ted breathes slowly, talks clearly.

"I don't go to school anymore, Dad. I'm grown up now."

"How did your essay go?"

"Sit down now, please, Dad. Sit down."

"You look scared, Ted. Why are you scared?"

"Don't worry, Dad. I was just . . . I . . . you can't go out in the boat. I've told you a thousand times. . . ."

They aren't in the garden anymore; they're in an odorless room with white walls. The dad lays his hand on the bearded cheek.

"Don't be scared, Ted. Do you remember when I taught you to fish? When we stayed in the tent out on the island and you had to sleep in my sleeping bag because you had a nightmare and wet yourself? Do you remember what I said to you? That it's good to wet yourself because it keeps the bears away. There's nothing wrong with being a bit scared."

When the dad sits down he lands on a soft bed, freshly made up by someone who isn't going to sleep there. This isn't his room. Ted is sitting next to him and the old man buries his nose in his son's hair.

"Do you remember, Ted? The tent on the island?"

"That wasn't me in the tent with you, Dad. It was Noah," the son whispers.

The dad lifts his head and stares at him.

"Who's Noah?"

Ted gently strokes his cheek.

"Noah, Dad. My son. You stayed in the tent with Noah. I don't like fishing."

"You do! I taught you! I taught you . . . didn't I teach you?"

"You never had time to teach me, Dad. You were always working. But you taught Noah, you've taught him everything. He's the one who loves math, like you."

The father's fingers grope around the bed; he's looking for something in his pockets, more and more frantically. When he sees that his boy has tears in his eyes, his own gaze flees toward the corner of the room. He clenches his fists until his knuckles turn white to stop them from shaking, mutters angrily:

"But what about school, Ted? Tell me how it's going at school!"

A boy and his grandpa are sitting on a bench in Grandpa's brain.

"It's such a nice brain, Grandpa," Noah says encouragingly, because Grandma always said that whenever Grandpa goes quiet, you just have to give him a compliment to get him going again.

"That's nice of you." Grandpa smiles and dries his eyes with the back of his hand.

"A bit messy though." The boy grins.

"It rained for a long time here when your Grandma died. I never quite got it back in order after that."

Noah notices that the ground beneath the bench has become muddy, but the keys and shards of glass are still there. Beyond the square is the lake, and small waves roll over it, memories of boats already passed. Noah can almost see the green tent on the island in the distance, remembers the fog which used to tenderly hug the trees like a cool sheet at dawn when they woke. Whenever Noah was scared of sleeping, Grandpa would take out a string and tie one end around his arm and the other around the boy's and promise that if Noah had nightmares he only had to pull on the string and Grandpa would wake up and bring him straight back to safety. Like a boat on a jetty. Grandpa kept his promise, every single time. Noah's legs dangle over the edge of the bench; the dragon has fallen asleep in the middle of the square, next to a fountain. There's a small group of tall buildings on the horizon on the other shore, amid the ruins of others which look like they've recently fallen down. The last ones standing are covered in blinking neon lights, strung here and there across their facades like they were taped up by someone who was either in too much of a hurry or absolutely desperate for a poo. They wink patterns through the fog, Noah realizes, forming letters. "Important!" one of the buildings twinkles. "Remember!" says another one. But on the very tallest building, the one closest to the beach, the lights say, "Pictures of Noah."

"What are those buildings, Grandpa?"

"They're archives. That's where everything is kept. All the most important things."

"Like what?"

"Everything we've done. All the photos and films and all your most unnecessary presents."

Grandpa laughs, Noah too. They always give each other unnecessary presents. Grandpa gave Noah a plastic bag full of air for Christmas and Noah gave Grandpa a sandal. For his birthday, Noah gave Grandpa a piece of chocolate he'd already eaten. That was Grandpa's favorite.

"That's a big building."

"It was a big piece of chocolate."

"Why are you holding my hand so tight, Grandpa?"

"Sorry, Noahnoah. Sorry."

The ground around the fountain in the square is covered in hard stone slabs. Someone has scrawled advanced mathematical calculations all over them in white chalk, but blurry people are rushing this way and that across them and the soles of their shoes rub away the numbers one by one until only random lines remain, carved deeply into the stones. Fossil equations. The dragon sneezes in its sleep; its nostrils send a million scraps of paper covered in handwritten messages flying across the square. A hundred elves from a book of fairy tales Grandma used to read to Noah dance around the fountain trying to catch them.

"What's on those pieces of paper?" the boy asks.

"Those are all my ideas," Grandpa replies.

"They're blowing away."

"They've been doing that for a long time."

The boy nods and wraps his fingers tightly around Grandpa's.

"Is your brain ill?"

"Who told you that?"

"Dad."

Grandpa exhales through his nose. Nods.

"We don't know, really. We know so little about how the brain works. It's like a fading star right now—do you remember what I taught you about that?"

"When a star fades it takes a long time for us to realize, as long as it takes for the last of its light to reach Earth."

Grandpa's chin trembles. He often reminds Noah that the universe is over thirteen billion years old. Grandma always used to mutter, "And you're still in such a hurry to look at it that you never have time to do the dishes." "Those who hasten to live are in a hurry to miss," she sometimes used to whisper to Noah, though he didn't know what she meant before she was buried. Grandpa clasps his hands to stop them from shaking.

"When a brain fades it takes a long time for the body to realize. The human body has a tremendous work ethic; it's a mathematical masterpiece, it'll keep working until the very last light. Our brains are the most boundless equation, and once humanity solves it it'll be more powerful than when we went to the moon. There's no greater mystery in the universe than a human. Do you remember what I told you about failing?"

"The only time you've failed is if you don't try once more."

"Exactly, Noahnoah, exactly. A great thought can never be kept on Earth."

Noah closes his eyes, stops the tears in their tracks, and forces them to cower beneath his eyelids. Snow starts to fall in the square, the same way very small children cry, like it had barely started at first but soon like it would never end. Heavy, white flakes cover all of Grandpa's ideas.

"Tell me about school, Noahnoah," the old man says.

He always wants to know everything about school, but not like other adults, who only want to know if Noah is behaving. Grandpa wants to know if the school is behaving. It hardly ever is.

"Our teacher made us write a story about what we want to be when we're big," Noah tells him.

"What did you write?"

"I wrote that I wanted to concentrate on being little first."

"That's a very good answer."

"Isn't it? I would rather be old than a grown-up. All grown-ups are angry, it's just children and old people who laugh."

"Did you write that?"

"Yes."

"What did your teacher say?"

"She said I hadn't understood the task."

"And what did you say?"

"I said she hadn't understood my answer."

"I love you," Grandpa manages to say with closed eyes.

"You're bleeding again," Noah says with his hand on Grandpa's forearm.

Grandpa wipes his forehead with a faded handkerchief. He's searching for something in his pockets. Then he looks at the boy's shoes, the way they swing a few inches above the tarmac with unruly shadows beneath them.

"When your feet touch the ground, I'll be in space, my dear Noahnoah."

The boy concentrates on breathing in time with Grandpa. That's another of their games.

"Are we here to learn how to say good-bye, Grandpa?" he eventually asks.

The old man scratches his chin, thinks for a long time.

"Yes, Noahnoah. I'm afraid we are."

"I think good-byes are hard," the boy admits.

Grandpa nods and strokes his cheek softly, though his fingertips are as rough as dry suede.

"You get that from your Grandma."

Noah remembers. When his dad picked him up from Grandma and Grandpa's in the evenings he wasn't even allowed to say those words to her. "Don't say it, Noah, don't you dare say it to me! I get old when you leave me. Every wrinkle on my face is a good-bye from you," she used to complain. And so he sang to her instead, and that made her laugh. She taught him to read and bake saffron buns and pour coffee without the pot dribbling, and when her hands started to shake the boy taught himself to pour half cups so she wouldn't spill any, because she was always ashamed when she did and he never let her feel ashamed in front of him. "The amount I love you, Noah," she would tell him with her lips to his ear after she read fairy tales about elves and he was just about to fall asleep, "the sky will never be that big." She wasn't perfect, but she was his. The boy sang to her the night before she died. Her body stopped working before her brain did. For Grandpa it's the opposite.

"I'm bad at good-byes," says the boy.

Grandpa's lips reveal all his teeth when he smiles.

"We'll have plenty of chances to practice. You'll be good at it. Almost all grown adults walk around full of regret over a good-bye they wish they'd been able to go back and say better. Our good-bye doesn't have to be like that, you'll be able to keep redoing it until it's perfect. And once it's perfect, that's when your feet will touch the ground and I'll be in space, and there won't be anything to be afraid of."

Noah holds the old man's hand, the man who taught

him to fish and to never be afraid of big thoughts and to look at the night's sky and understand that it's made of numbers. Mathematics has blessed the boy in that sense, because he's no longer afraid of the thing almost everyone else is terrified of: infinity. Noah loves space because it never ends. It never dies. It's the one thing in his life which won't ever leave him.

He swings his legs, studies the glittering metals between the flowers.

"There are numbers on all the keys, Grandpa."

Grandpa leans forward over the edge and calmly looks at them.

"Yes, indeed, there are."

"Why?"

"I can't remember."

He suddenly sounds so afraid. His body is heavy, his voice is weak, and his skin is a sail about to be abandoned by the wind.

"Why are you holding my hand so tight, Grandpa?" the boy whispers again.

"Because all of this is disappearing, Noahnoah. And I want to keep hold of you longest of all."

The boy nods. Holds his grandpa's hand tighter in return.

He holds the girl's hand tighter and tighter and tighter, until she tenderly loosens one finger after another and kisses him on the neck.

"You're squeezing me like I was a rope."

"I don't want to lose you again. I couldn't go on."

She walks lightheartedly along the road next to him.

"I'm here. I've always been here. Tell me more about Noah, tell me everything."

His face softens bit by bit, until he's grinning and replies:

"He's so tall now, his feet are going to reach all the way to the ground soon."

"You'll have to put more stones under the anchor then," she says with a laugh.

His lungs force him to stop and lean against a tree. Their names are carved into the bark, but he doesn't remember why.

"My memories are running away from me, my love, like when you try to separate oil and water. I'm constantly reading a book with a missing page, and it's always the most important one."

"I know, I know you're afraid," she answers and brushes her lips against his cheek.

"Where is this road taking us?"

"Home," she replies.

"Where are we?"

"We're back where we met. The dance hall where you stepped on my toes is over there, the café where I accidentally trapped your hand in the door. Your little finger is still crooked, you used to say that I probably only married you because I felt bad about that."

"I didn't care why you said yes. Just that you stayed."

"There's the church where you became mine. There's the house that became ours."

He closes his eyes, lets his nose lead the way.

"Your hyacinths. They've never smelled so strong."

For more than half a century they belonged to one another. She detested the same characteristics in him that last day as she had the first time she saw him under that tree, and still adored all the others.

"When you looked straight at me when I was seventy I fell just as hard as I did when I was sixteen." She smiles.

His fingertips touch the skin above her collarbone.

"You never became ordinary to me, my love. You were electric shocks and fire."

Her teeth tickle his earlobe when she replies:

"No one could ask for more."

No one had ever fought with him like she had. Their very first fight had been about the universe; he explained how it had been created and she refused to accept it. He raised his voice, she got angry, he couldn't understand why, and she shouted, "I'm angry because you think everything happened by chance but there are billions of people on this planet and I found *you* so if you're saying I could just as well have found someone else then I can't bear your bloody mathematics!" Her fists had been clenched. He stood there looking at her for several minutes. Then he said that he loved her. It was the first time. They never stopped arguing and they never slept apart; he spent an entire working life calculating probabilities and she was the most improbable person he ever met. She turned him upside-down.

When they moved into their first house he spent the dark months growing a garden so beautiful that it knocked the air out of her when the light finally came. He did it with a determination only science can mobilize in a grown man, because he wanted to show that mathematics could be beautiful. He measured the angles of the sun, drew diagrams of where the trees cast their shade, kept statistics for the day-to-day temperatures, and optimized the choice of plants. "I wanted you to know," he said as she stood barefoot in the grass that June and cried. "Know what?" she asked. "That equations are magic, and that all formulas are spells," he said.

Now they are old and on a road. Her words against the fabric of his shirt:

"And then you went about growing coriander in secret every year, just to mess with me."

He throws out his arms in a gesture of innocence:

"I don't know what you're talking about. I forget things, you know, I'm an old man. Are you saying you don't like coriander?"

"You've always known I hate it!"

"It must've been Noah. There's no trusting that boy." He laughs.

She stands on her tiptoes with both hands clutching his shirt and fixes her eyes on him.

"You were never easy, darling difficult sulky you, never diplomatic. You might even have been easy to dislike at times. But no one, absolutely no one, would dare tell me you were hard to love."

Next to the garden, which smelled of hyacinths and sometimes coriander, there was an old field. And there, right on the other side of the hedge, was a broken old fishing boat dragged up onto land by a neighbor many years earlier. Grandpa always said that he couldn't get any peace and quiet when he worked in the house, and Grandma always replied that she couldn't get any peace and quiet in the house when Grandpa was working there, so one morning Grandma went out into the garden and around the hedge and started to decorate the boat's cabin as an office. Grandpa sat there for years after that, surrounded by numbers and calculations and equations; it was the only place on Earth where everything was logical to him. Mathematicians need a place like that. Maybe everyone else does too.

There was a huge anchor leaning against one side of the boat. When Ted was very small, the boy would occasionally ask his dad how long it would be before he was taller than it. The dad has tried to remember when it happened. He's tried so hard that the square in his head quaked. He learned his lesson; he was a different man when Noah was born, became someone else as Grandpa than he had been as a father. That's not unique to mathematicians. When Noah asked the same question Ted once had, Grandpa replied, "You'll have to hope it never happens, because only people who are shorter than the anchor get to play in my office whenever they want." And when Noah's head began to approach the top of the anchor, Grandpa placed stones beneath it so he would never lose the privilege of being disturbed.

"Noah has gotten so smart, my love."

"He always has been, it just took you awhile to catch up," she snorts.

His voice catches in his throat.

"My brain is shrinking now, the square gets smaller every night."

She strokes his temples.

"Do you remember what you said, when we first fell in love, that sleeping was a torment?"

"Yes. Because we couldn't share our sleep. Every morning when I blinked awake, the seconds before I knew where I was were unbearable. Until I knew where you were."

She kisses him.

"I know that the way home is getting longer and longer every morning. But I loved you because your brain, your world, was always bigger than everyone else's. There's still a lot of it left."

"I miss you unbearably."

She smiles, her tears on his face.

"Darling stubborn you. I know you never believed in life after death. But you should know that I'm dearly, dearly, dearly hoping that you're wrong."

The road behind her is blurry, the horizon bearing rain. He holds her as hard as he can. Sighs deeply.

"Lord how you'll argue with me then. If we meet in Heaven."

A rake has been left propped against a wall. Lying next to it are three plant markers flecked with damp earth. On the ground, there's a bag with a pair of glasses sticking out of one of its pockets. A microscope has been forgotten on a footstool and there's a white coat hanging from a hook, a pair of red shoes visible beneath. Grandpa proposed to her here, by the fountain, and Grandma's things are still everywhere.

The boy carefully touches the lump on Grandpa's forehead.

"Does it hurt?" he asks.

"No, not really," Grandpa replies.

"I mean on the inside. Does it hurt on the inside?"

"It hurts less and less. That's one good thing about

forgetting things. You forget the things that hurt too."

"What does it feel like?"

"Like constantly searching for something in your pockets. First you lose the small things, then it's the big ones. It starts with keys and ends with people."

"Are you scared?"

"A bit. Are you?"

"A bit," the boy admits.

Grandpa grins.

"That'll keep the bears away."

Noah's cheek is resting against the old man's collarbone.

"When you've forgotten a person, do you forget you've forgotten?"

"No, sometimes I remember that I've forgotten. That's the worst kind of forgetting. Like being locked out in a storm. Then I try to force myself to remember harder, so hard that the whole square here shakes."

"Is that why you get so tired?"

"Yes, sometimes it feels like having fallen asleep on a sofa while it's still light and then suddenly being woken up once it's dark; it takes me a few seconds to remember where I am. I'm in space for a few moments, have to blink and rub my eyes and let my brain take a couple of extra steps to remember who I am and where I am. To get home. That's the road that's getting longer and longer every morning, the way home from space. I'm sailing on a big calm lake, Noahnoah."

"Horrible," says the boy.

"Yes. Very, very, very horrible. For some reason places and directions seem to be the first thing to disappear. First you forget where you're going, then where you've been, and eventually where you are . . . or . . . maybe it was the other way around. . . . I . . . my doctor said something. I went to my doctor and he said something about it, or did I say something. I said: 'Doctor, I . . .'"

He raps his temples, harder and harder. The square moves.

"It doesn't matter," the boy whispers.

"Sorry, Noahnoah."

The boy strokes his arm, shrugs.

"Don't worry. I'm going to give you a balloon, Grandpa. So you can have it in space."

"A balloon won't stop me from disappearing, Noahnoah." Grandpa sighs.

"I know. But you'll get it on your birthday. As a present."

"That sounds unnecessary." Grandpa smiles.

The boy nods.

"If you keep hold of it you'll know that right before you went into space someone gave you a balloon. And it's the most unnecessary present anyone can get because there's absolutely *no* need for a balloon in space. And that'll make you laugh."

Grandpa closes his eyes. Breathes in the boy's hair.

"That's the best present I've never been given."

The lake glitters, their feet move from side to side,

trouser legs fluttering in the wind. It smells like water and sunshine on the bench. Not everyone knows that water and sunshine have scents, but they do, you just have to get far enough away from all other smells to realize it. You have to be sitting still in a boat, relaxing so much that you have time to lie on your back and think. Lakes and thoughts have that in common, they take time. Grandpa leans toward Noah and breathes out like people do at the start of a long sleep; one of them is getting bigger and one of them is getting smaller, the years allow them to meet in the middle. The boy points to a road on the other side of the square, blocked off by a barrier and a big warning sign.

"What's happened there, Grandpa?"

Grandpa blinks several times with his head against the boy's collarbone.

"Oh . . . that road . . . I think it's . . . it's closed. It washed away in the rain when your Grandma died. It's too dangerous to think about now, Noahnoah."

"Where did it go?"

"It was a shortcut. It didn't take long at all to get home in the mornings when I took that road, I just woke up and there I was," Grandpa mumbles and raps his forehead.

The boy wants to ask more, but Grandpa manages to stop him.

"Tell me more about school, Noahnoah."

Noah shrugs.

"We don't count enough and we write too much."

"That's always the way. They never learn, the schools."

"And I don't like the music lessons. Dad's trying to teach me to play guitar, but I can't."

"Don't worry. People like us have a different kind of music, Noahnoah."

"And we have to write essays all the time! The teacher wanted us to write what we thought the meaning of life was once."

"What did you write?"

"Company."

Grandpa closes his eyes.

"That's the best answer I've heard."

"My teacher said I had to write a longer answer."

"So what did you do?"

"I wrote: Company. And ice cream."

Grandpa spends a moment or two thinking that over.
Then he asks:

"What kind of ice cream?"

Noah smiles. It's nice to be understood.

He and the girl are on a road and they're young again. He remembers each of the very first times he saw her, he hides those pictures as far from the rain as he can. They were sixteen and even the snow was happy that morning, falling soap-bubble light and landing on cold cheeks as though the flakes were gently trying to wake someone they loved. She stood in front of him with January in her hair and he was lost. She was the first person in his life that he couldn't work out, though he spent every minute of it after that day trying.

"I always knew who I was with you. You were my shortcut," Grandpa confides.

"Even though I never had any sense of direction." She laughs.

"Death isn't fair."

"No, death is a slow drum. It counts every beat. We can't haggle with it for more time."

"Beautifully said, my love."

"I stole it."

Their laughter echoes in each other's chests, and then he says:

"I miss all our most ordinary things. Breakfast on the veranda. Weeds in the flower beds."

She takes a breath, then answers:

"I miss the dawn. The way it stamped its feet at the end of the water, increasingly frustrated and impatient, until there was no more holding back the sun. The way it sparkled right across the lake, reached the stones by the jetty and came onto land, its warm hands in our garden, pouring gentle light into our house, letting us kick off the covers and start the day. I miss you then, darling sleepy you. Miss you there."

"We lived an extraordinarily ordinary life."

"An ordinarily extraordinary life."

She laughs. Old eyes, new sunlight, and he still remembers how it felt to fall in love. The rain hasn't arrived yet.

They dance on the shortcut until darkness falls.

People are moving back and forth across the square. A blurry man steps on the dragon's foot, the dragon gives him a telling off. A boy is playing guitar beneath a tree, a sad tune, Grandpa hums along. A young woman walks barefoot across the square, stops to stroke the dragon. Her palms suddenly search her

red coat, finding something in her pockets, something she seems to have spent a long time looking for. She looks up, straight at Noah, laughs happily and waves. As though he helped her to look, and she wants him to know he can stop now. That she's found it. That everything's okay. For a single moment he sees her face clearly. She has Grandma's eyes. Then the boy blinks, and she's gone.

"She looked like . . ." he whispers.

"I know." Grandpa nods, his hands move anxiously in his own pockets, then he lifts them up and lets his fingers move against his temples, like the outside of a box of raisins. Like he's trying to shake loose a piece of the past in there.

"I . . . she . . . that's your grandma. She was younger. You never got to meet her young, she has . . . she had the strongest feelings I ever experienced in a person, when she got angry she could empty a full bar of grown men, and when she was happy . . . there was no defending yourself against that, Noahnoah. She was a force of nature. Everything I am came from her, she was my Big Bang."

"How did you fall in love with her?" the boy asks.

Grandpa's hands land with one palm on his own knee and one on the boy's.

"She got lost in my heart, I think. Couldn't find her way out. Your grandma always had a terrible sense of direction. She could get lost on an escalator."

And then comes his laughter, crackling and popping like it's smoke from dry wood in his stomach. He puts an arm around the boy.

"Never in my life have I asked myself how I fell in love with her, Noahnoah. Only the other way around."

The boy looks at the keys on the ground, at the square and the fountain. He glances up toward space; if he stretches his fingers he can touch it. It's soft. When he and Grandpa go fishing they sometimes lie in the bottom of the boat with their eyes closed for hours without saying a word to one another. When Grandma was here she always stayed at home, and if anyone asked where her husband and grandson were she always said, "Space." It belongs to them.

It was a morning in December when she died. The whole house smelled of hyacinths and the boy cried the whole day. That night he lay next to Grandpa on his back in the snow in the garden and looked up at the stars. They sang for Grandma, both of them. Sang for space. Have done the same almost every night since. She belongs to them.

"Are you scared you're going to forget her?" the boy asks.

Grandpa nods.

"Very."

"Maybe you just need to forget her funeral," the boy suggests.

The boy himself could well imagine forgetting funerals. All funerals. But Grandpa shakes his head.

"If I forget the funeral I'll forget why I can't ever forget her."

"That sounds messy."

"Life sometimes is."

"Grandma believed in God, but you don't. Do you still get to go to Heaven if you die?"

"Only if I'm wrong."

The boy bites his lip and makes a promise:

"I'll tell you about her when you forget, Grandpa. First thing every morning, first of all I'll tell you about her."

Grandpa squeezes his arm.

"Tell me that we danced, Noahnoah. Tell me that that's what it's like to fall in love, like you don't have room for yourself in your own feet."

"I promise."

"And tell me that she hated coriander. Tell me that I used to tell waiters in restaurants that she had a serious allergy, and when they asked whether someone could really be allergic to coriander I said: 'Believe me, she's seriously allergic, if you serve her coriander she could die!' She didn't find that funny at all, she said, but she laughed when she thought I wasn't looking."

"She used to say that coriander was a punishment rather than a herb." Noah laughs.

Grandpa nods, blinks at the treetops, and takes deep breaths from the leaves. Then he rests his forehead against the boy's and says:

"Noahnoah, promise me something, one very last thing: once your good-bye is perfect, you have to leave me and not look back. Live your life. It's an awful thing to miss someone who's still here."

The boy spends a long time thinking about that. Then he says:

"But one good thing with your brain being sick is that you're going to be really good at keeping secrets. That's a good thing if you're a grandpa."

Grandpa nods.

"That's true, that's true . . . what was that?"

Both of them grin.

"And I don't think you need to be scared of forgetting me," the boy says after a moment's consideration.

"No?"

The corners of the boy's mouth reach his earlobes.

"No. Because if you forget me then you'll just get the chance to get to know me again. And you'll like that, because I'm actually a pretty cool person to get to know."

Grandpa laughs and the square shakes. He knows no greater blessing.

They're sitting on the grass, him and her.

"Ted is so angry at me, love," Grandpa says.

"He's not angry at you, he's angry at the universe. He's angry because your enemy isn't something he can fight."

"It's a big universe to be angry with, a never-ending fury. I wish that he . . ."

"That he was more like you?"

"Less. That he was less like me. Less angry."

"He is. Just sadder. Do you remember when he was little and asked you why people went into space?"

"Yes. I told him it was because people are born adventurers, we have to explore and discover, it's our nature."

"But you could see that he was scared, so you also said: 'Ted, we're not going into space because we're afraid of aliens. We're going because we're scared we're alone. It's an awfully big universe to be alone in.'"

"Did I say that? That was smart of me."

"You probably stole it from someone."

"Probably."

"Ted might say the same thing to Noah now."

"Noah has never been afraid of space."

"That's because Noah is like me, he believes in God."

The old man lies down on the grass and smiles at the

trees. She gets up and walks past the hedge, along the side of the boat, stroking it thoughtfully.

"Don't forget to put more stones under the anchor, Noah is growing so quickly," she reminds him.

The boat's cabin, the room in which he worked for so many years, looks so small in the twilight. Even though there was space for all his biggest thoughts. The lights are still there, the ones he strung up in a tangle on the outside of the boat so that Noah could always find his way if he woke up from a nightmare and needed to find his grandpa. A chaotic mess of green, yellow, and purple bulbs, as though Grandpa had been desperate for a poo when he put them up, so Noah would start laughing when he saw them. You can't be afraid of crossing dark gardens if you're laughing.

She lies down next to him, sighs with his skin close to hers.

"This is where we built our life. Everything. There's the road where you taught Ted to ride a bike."

His lips vanish between his teeth when he admits:

"Ted taught himself. Like he taught himself to play guitar after I told him to stop messing about with it and do his homework instead."

"You were a busy man," she whispers, regret filling every word because she knows she bears the same guilt.

"And now Ted is a busy man," he says.

"But the universe gave you both Noah. He's the bridge between you. That's why we get the chance to spoil our grandchildren, because by doing that we're apologizing to our children."

"And how do we stop our children from hating us for that?"

"We can't. That's not our job."

He chases his breaths between throat and chest.

"Everyone always wondered how you put up with me, my love. Sometimes I wonder too."

Her giggles, how he misses them, the way they seemed to gain speed all the way from her feet.

"You were the first boy I met who knew how to dance. I thought it was probably best to seize the opportunity; who knows how often boys like that turn up?"

"I'm sorry about the coriander."

"No you're not, not at all."

"No, not at all, actually."

She carefully lets go of his hand in the darkness, but her voice still rests in his ear.

"Don't forget to put more stones under the anchor. And ask Ted about the guitar."

"It's too late now."

She laughs inside his brain then.

"Darling obstinate you. It's never too late to ask your son about something he loves."

Then the rain starts to fall, and the last thing he shouts to her is that he also hopes he's wrong. Dearly, dearly, dearly hopes. That she'll argue with him in Heaven.

A boy and his dad walk down a corridor; the dad holds the boy's hand softly.

"It's okay to be afraid, Noah, you don't need to be ashamed," he repeats.

"I know, Dad, don't worry," Noah says and yanks up his trousers when they slip down.

"They're a little bit too big; that was the smallest size they had. I'll have to adjust them for you when we get home," the dad promises.

"Is Grandpa in pain?" Noah wants to know.

"No, don't worry about that, he just cut his head when he fell over in the boat. It looks worse than it is, but he's not in pain, Noah."

"I mean on the inside. Does it hurt on the inside?"

The dad is breathing through his nose, and his eyes are closed; his steps slow down.

"It's hard to explain, Noah."

Noah nods and holds his hand more tightly.

"Don't be scared, Dad. It'll keep the bears away."

"What will?"

"Me wetting myself in the ambulance. That'll keep the bears away. There won't be any bears in that ambulance for years!"

Noah's dad's laugh is like a rumble. Noah loves it. Those big hands gently holding his small ones.

"We just need to be careful, does that make sense? With your grandpa. His brain . . . the thing is, Noah, sometimes it's going to be working slower than we're used to. Slower than Grandpa is used to."

"Yeah. The way home's getting longer and longer every morning now."

The father squats down and hugs him.

"My wonderful smart little boy. The amount I love you, Noah, the sky will never be that big."

"What can we do to help Grandpa?"

The dad's tears dry on the boy's sweatshirt.

"We can walk down the road with him. We can keep him company."

They take the lift down to the hospital parking lot, walk hand in hand toward the car. Fetch the green tent.

Ted and his dad are arguing again. Ted begs him to sit down, the dad furiously bellows:

"I don't have time to teach you to ride your bike today, Ted! I told you! I have to work!"

"It's okay, Dad. I know."

"For God's sake, I just want my cigarettes! Tell me where you've hidden my cigarettes!" the dad roars.

"You stopped smoking years ago," says Ted.

"How the hell would you know?"

"I know because you stopped when I was born, Dad."

They stare at one another and breathe. Breathe and breathe and breathe. It's a never-ending rage, being angry at the universe.

"I . . . it . . ." Grandpa mumbles.

Ted's big hands hold his thin shoulders; Grandpa touches his beard.

"You've gotten so big, Tedted."

"Dad, listen to me, Noah is here now. He's going to sit with you. I just need to get a few things from the car."

Grandpa nods and rests his forehead against Ted's forehead.

"We need to go home soon, my boy, your mother's waiting for us. I'm sure she's worried."

Ted bites his lower lip.

"Okay, Dad. Soon. Really, really soon."

"How tall are you now, Tedted?"

"Six foot one, Dad."

"We'll have to put more stones under the anchor when we get home."

Ted is almost at the door when Grandpa asks if he has his guitar with him.

There's a hospital room at the end of a life where someone, right in the middle of the floor, has pitched a green tent. A person wakes up inside it, breathless and afraid, not knowing where he is. A young man sitting next to him whispers:

"Don't be scared."

The person sits up in his sleeping bag, hugs his shaking knees, cries.

"Don't be scared," the young man repeats.

A balloon bounces against the roof of the tent; its string reaches the person's fingertips.

"I don't know who you are," he whispers.

The young man strokes his forearm.

"I'm Noah. You're my grandpa. You taught me to cycle on the road outside your house and you loved my grandma so much that there wasn't room for you in your own feet. She hated coriander but put up with you. You swore you would never stop smoking but you did when you became a father. You've been to space, because you're a born adventurer, and once you went to your doctor and said, 'Doctor, doctor! I've broken my arm in two places!' and then the doctor told you that you should really stop going there."

Grandpa smiles then, without moving his lips. Noah places the string from the balloon in his hand and shows him how he is holding the other end.

"We're inside the tent we used to sleep in by the lake, Grandpa, do you remember? If you tie this string around your wrist you can keep hold of the balloon when you fall asleep, and when you get scared you just need to yank it and I'll pull you back. Every time."

Grandpa nods slowly and strokes Noah's cheek in wonder.

"You look different, Noahnoah. How is school? Are the teachers better now?"

"Yes, Grandpa, the teachers are better. I'm one of them now. The teachers are great now."

"That's good, that's good, Noahnoah, a great brain can never be kept on Earth," Grandpa whispers and closes his eyes.

Space sings outside the hospital room; Ted plays guitar; Grandpa hums along. It's a big universe to be angry at but a long life to have company in. Noah strokes his daughter's hair; the girl turns toward him in the sleeping bag without waking up. She doesn't like mathematics, she prefers words and instruments like her grandpa. It won't be long before her feet touch the ground. They sleep in a row, the tent smells like hyacinths, and there's nothing to be afraid of.

SEBASTIAN AND THE TROLL

a little story about how it feels

S ebastian lives in a bubble of glass. This is a problem, of course, on this everybody on the outside agrees. Glass bubbles are very impractical, for example, in classrooms and at birthday parties. In the beginning everybody thought the glass was the problem, but after he'd lived in there long enough it was decided instead that Sebastian was the problem. The people on the outside say you can't establish eye contact with him, that he seems "absent," as if where he is somehow is worth less than where they are.

"Don't you want to go outside in the fresh air and play ball? Wouldn't that be fun?" they used to ask when he was little and their voices could still be heard all the way in. He couldn't explain then that he didn't think having fun seemed liked fun. That being happy didn't make him happy. He can't remember the last time any of them said something funny and he laughed. Maybe he never has, and in that case they're probably right, the people who, for as long as he can remember, have been shaking their heads and saying, "There's something wrong with him," to Sebastian's parents.

He sat close to the glass back then, reading the words off their lips. They were right. A person is supposed to think that having fun *is* fun, otherwise something that shouldn't be broken is broken. Something that isn't broken in children who aren't weird. For years, various grown-ups came and went outside the bubble. Some carefully tapped the glass, others banged it hard when he didn't answer. Some asked him how he "felt." He wanted to tell them that it feels like feeling nothing, yet still it hurts. Some said Sebastian "suffers from depression," but they said it as though they were the ones actually suffering. Sebastian himself said nothing, and now he can't hear anyone at all from the outside anymore. He doesn't know if it's because they gave up or if the glass just got thicker.

When the bubble still had tiny openings at the top

they dropped down little pills. They said the pills were supposed to make the glass thinner, but he thinks they might have misunderstood. He's not sure they know as much about glass as they claim. The pills got stuck and blocked the last few openings. Now there's only Sebastian in here.

He can't sleep at night. Sometimes his parents can't either. He can see their tears run slowly down the outside of the glass then. They sound like rain over rooftops. Sebastian knows that his parents wish that something awful had happened to him. Because then there'd be a reason for him to hurt. Then he could be understood, maybe even fixed. But Sebastian's darkness is not just a light switch that someone forgot to flip, not just a pill he doesn't want to take. His darkness is a heaviness and a tiredness that pulls the bones of his chest inwards and downwards until he can't breathe. And now the bubble's gotten bigger, or maybe Sebastian has gotten smaller. Maybe that's what anxiety does to us, shrinks us. He sometimes falls asleep in the afternoons from ex-haustion, not tiredness. Sleeps with shallow breaths and deep nightmares, just for a few minutes at a time. Until he wakes up one evening with fur in his eyes.

There is a troll sitting in his bubble.

Sebastian knows it's a troll since he asks the troll:

"What are you?"

And the troll replies:

"A troll."

Then you know. But Sebastian still needs to ask:

"What do you mean, 'a troll?'"

The troll is busy, it's concentrated on writing some-thing on tiny white notes with a nice blue pen. More and more and more white notes are stacked in uneven piles everywhere, until the troll looks up at Sebastian. "Regu-lar kind of troll," it says, since that's what it is. Nothing special for a troll, but special since it is a troll, of course. After all, it's not that often you see a troll, either in a bubble or anywhere else.

"What are you writing on the notes?" Sebastian asks.

"Your name," the troll answers.

"Why?"

"So that you don't forget that you are somebody."

Sebastian doesn't know how to reply to that. So he says:

"Nice pen."

"It's the most beautiful pen I know, I always carry it with me because I want them to know that I love them," the troll says.

"Who?"

"The letters."

Sebastian's fingertips touch the glass of the bubble.

"How did you get in here?" he asks.

"I didn't get in, I got out," the troll says and stretches sleepily.

"From what?"

"From you. Through one of the cracks."

"I've cracked?"

The troll rolls its eyes, disgruntledly flails its paw against the walls of the bubble, kicks a threshold, annoyed. Sebastian didn't even know there were thresholds in here.

"You see, this here shack won't do anymore, Sebastian. The glass has gotten too thick and everything that's in here hurts too much. In the end, there'll be no air left and then something has to crack. Either the bubble or you."

Sebastian's fingers fumble over his stomach. His throat. His face. Small, tiny cracks everywhere. They don't hurt. Sebastian thinks that maybe he's forgotten how to do it, how to hurt in places where other people hurt in all the normal ways. Burn-your-hand-on-a-hot-pan ways. Stub-your-toe-on-furniture ways. Now he only hurts in weird ways. Ways-that-don't-leave-a-scar ways. Ways-that-can't-be-seen-on-an-X-ray ways.

"How did you fit inside me?" he asks the troll.

"Oh, it wasn't hard at all. I've been asleep inside

your heart for a hundred thousand years. Trolls get very small when we sleep. Like balloons, balloons also become very small when they sleep."

"And when they break," Sebastian notes.

The troll nods thoughtfully, as if this is very, very true. Then asks:

"Is there breakfast?"

Sebastian shakes his head. He doesn't eat very much anymore, everyone worries about that, as if food were the problem instead of the problem being the problem. It's easier to worry about food, of course; it's understandable that the people on the outside stick to the kind of worrying they know best. The troll looks very disappointed.

"You get pretty hungry after a hundred thousand years. Breakfast would have been nice."

"I'm sorry," Sebastian says.

The troll nods, with sorrow in its eyes.

"I know, Sebastian. I know how sad you are."

Sebastian reaches his hand out. The troll is soft, its fur thick.

"You're not from my imagination. My imagination isn't this good."

The troll takes a deep bow.

"Thank you."

"What do you want from me?" Sebastian asks.

"What do you want for you?" the troll asks.

"I want it to stop hurting," Sebastian says.

"What?" the troll asks.

"You should know, if you've been inside me. Everything. I want everything to stop hurting," Sebastian begs.

The troll doesn't lie to him then. Sebastian really likes the troll for that.

"I can't teach you how to make it stop hurting, Sebastian."

"Then what can you teach me?" Sebastian breathes in reply.

"How to fight."

"Fight against what?"

"Against everybody that's coming tonight."

"Who?"

"Your nightmares. Your weaknesses. Your inadequacies. Your monsters."

And at night, they come. All of them.

Sebastian sees them on the horizon of the bubble. They wait for a moment, just long enough for him to have time to be terrified. They love when he's terrified. And then they come, everyone that hurts, every nameless terror, everything Sebastian has ever feared. Every monster from under every bed and every creature from the darkest rooms inside his head. They ride straight towards the boy and the troll now, all the anxiety that there's space for in a child. Children always have so much more space inside them than grown-ups can remember.

Sebastian turns to run, but he's at the edge of a cliff, a hundred thousand feet high. The ground shakes; in a few seconds they'll be here, all his inner demons. He feels their shadows and how cold they make everything. He's cold on the inside now, the way you get when some of your skin is exposed to the air outside of the duvet on an early morning in November, just after winter has wrestled its way into autumn but before the radiators have had time to adjust. Sebastian spins around at the edge of the cliff with his palms open, like he's looking for heat, and suddenly he actually feels it. It's coming from below. If he jumps now he'll land in a bed, soft and safe and full of blankets, just the right size for pulling over the head of an average-size boy. He can see it from here. The demons hiss and snarl so close to the edge that the troll has to scream for Sebastian to hear it:

"They want you to do it!"

"Do what?" Sebastian roars, leaning over the edge.

He wonders whether it's really possible for anything to be worse down there than up here.

"They want you to jump, Sebastian!" the troll screams.

And Sebastian almost jumps. Because he knows how good it would feel on the way down, and then maybe it doesn't hurt anymore? Down there at the end of the falling down, maybe it will feel like it never hurt at all?

But the troll holds on to Sebastian's hand. Its paw is also soft. It can't be imagination, Sebastian thinks, because he doesn't have that good of an imagination and he knows practically nothing about paws, does he? So he stays, and everything that hurts rushes straight through him, down into the abyss, laughing and howling.

"They can't hurt you, not really, so they have to make you hurt yourself," the troll whispers.

Sebastian stands at the edge, out of breath.

"Are you sure?" he wonders.

"Are you sure there's no breakfast?" the troll asks.

"What do you mean?"

"I mean that sometimes you think you're sure of something, but that doesn't mean that you can't be wrong. You could for example see a balloon and be sure that someone dropped it, but it might actually have run away."

Sebastian starts hurting just behind his eyes.

"So you mean that you're . . . sure or not sure?"

The troll scratches a few different spots of fur.

"I just mean that breakfast would have been nice."

Sebastian apologizes, the troll nods disappointedly. Everything goes quiet. Then Sebastian's feet start moving, without him being involved. The bubble starts rocking, at first almost nothing at all but then almost immediately all at once. Sebastian closes his eyes and holds his knees with his hands, because there's nothing else to hold on to in here. He wants to throw up, but the troll places its paw on the back of his neck and then for a long while it feels like Sebastian takes off and floats.

"Watch out," the troll whispers, but Sebastian doesn't react until the troll yells, "WATCH OUT!"

All of a sudden Sebastian gets water up his nose. Then in his eyes. He flails his arms wildly, feels his clothes get wet and his shoes fill up with sharp claws. Something is pulling him down into the depths as if he's drowning. HE'S DROWNING!

"Did you push . . . you idiot . . . did you push me into . . . the ocean?" he screams to the troll, panicking with his nose barely above the surface.

"No, this isn't an . . . ocean, it's a . . . rain," the troll pants.

They both gasp for air. The sky disappears behind huge waves that pound and splash them on purpose, hurt them just because they can. The troll's fur gets dark and heavy and he is sucked into the depth. Sebastian reaches his hand out and grabs its paw, an endless storm riding in over them.

"Where did the rain come from?" Sebastian yells in the troll's ear, or at least where he thinks trolls might have ears.

"It's tears!" the troll roars back, where the troll thinks Sebastian has ears.

"Whose?"

"Yours! All the ones you've held back inside you! I told you, I TOLD YOU!!!"

"WHAT!?"

"THAT EITHER THE BUBBLE WILL CRACK! OR YOU WILL!"

Sebastian disappears under the surface, just for a few moments or maybe an entire life, before he struggles his way back up again. A flock of huge grey birds hover over them. Now and then they dive towards the water and snap at Sebastian's shirt collar. He shields himself with his arm, their sharp beaks leaving long, deep, bleeding cuts in him.

"Are they trying to . . . take me?" Sebastian screams with the rain and the wind raging and roaring across his cheeks.

"No, they're trying to . . . scare you!" the troll cries back while one of the birds takes off with a beakful of fur.

"Why?"

"Because they want you to stop swimming."

Sebastian grips tightly on to the troll's fur, closes his eyes even tighter. He doesn't know who is keeping whom afloat in the end. They're hurled through the waters, down into the darkness, into a wall. They land in a petrifying silence, impossible to trust. But at last Sebastian opens his eyes again and realizes that the two of them are lying coughing and snorting in the sand on a beach. The sun slowly dries fur and skin.

"Where are we?" Sebastian asks.

"At the bottom," the troll whispers.

"The bottom of what?"

"The bottom of you."

Sebastian sits up. He's got sand inside his clothes, in every place you don't want sand to be, and some places where Sebastian imagines that the sand wants to be just as little as Sebastian wants it there. It's warm when he lifts it up in his palms, runs around his fingers until it finds its way between them. Sebastian looks at his knuckles, full of cracks that don't hurt, and it's not raining anymore. Maybe it never rains at the bottom, maybe the sun always rests on you here, never too much and never too little. Surrounding the beach are high, smooth cliffs, impossible to climb. This is a paradise, at the bottom of a hole. Along one of the cliff faces there is a rope, and at its very end there's a campfire burning. Sebastian carefully opens his palms towards the small, bouncing flames to feel the heat. The wind tickles his ear.

"Do it," the wind shouts. "Do it!"

Sebastian scratches his ear, looks at the troll in surprise. The troll points sadly to the fire.

"Everyone is waiting for you to do it, Sebastian."

"What?"

"Decide that it's easier to stay down here. And set fire to the rope."

Sebastian blinks like his eyelashes have gotten stuck

to his heart and have to be ripped from it every time his eyes open.

"I can't live on the outside of the bubble," he stammers at last.

"You can't live in here either," the troll replies.

The words shiver when the answer falls from Sebastian's lips and the tears bring him to his knees:

"I don't want it to hurt anymore. Does everybody else hurt like this?"

"I don't know," the troll admits.

"Why do I hurt when nothing has happened? I never laugh! Everybody normal laughs!"

The troll's paws rub the spot where the troll probably has temples.

"Maybe it's your laugh that's broken. Not you. Maybe someone broke it. One time someone broke my favorite breakfast plate. I'm still a bit upset about it, actually."

"How do you fix a laugh?" Sebastian whispers.

"I don't know," the troll admits.

"What if there's something wrong with me after all?"

The troll looks to be taking this under serious consideration.

"Maybe something's wrong with the wrong?"

"Huh?"

"Maybe the balloon isn't even a balloon. Maybe you don't have to be happy. Maybe you just have to be."

"Be what?"

The troll writes something in the sand. Slowly and carefully, with its most beautiful letters. Then it promises:

"Just that."

The troll dries the boy's eyes. The boy asks:

"What do we do now?"

"Sleep," the troll suggests.

"Why?" the boy asks.

"Because sometimes when you wake up there's breakfast."

The troll puts its paw under Sebastian's cheek. Sebastian crawls up in it and falls asleep. From tiredness, not exhaustion. The troll sleeps around him, the boy's tears rest like crystals in its fur. When they wake up, the fire has gone out. Sebastian blinks at the sky.

"What are you thinking about?" the troll asks.

"I'm thinking that maybe the balloon was neither dropped nor ran away. Maybe someone just let it go," the boy whispers.

"Why would anyone let go of a balloon?" the troll asks.

"Because somebody wanted it to be happy."

The troll nods gratefully, as if this new thought is a little gift. Sebastian stretches forward carefully and touches the rope.

"What's up there?" he asks and points to the top of the cliffs where the rope is attached.

"A life. A hundred thousand years of all the best and all the worst," the troll whispers.

"And in-between that?"

The troll smiles, almost happily.

"Oh, yes! THAT! All the in-between. You get to choose that. The best and the worst in life just happens to us, but the in-between . . . that's what keeps us going."

Sebastian's breath bounces around in his throat.

"Will you come with me?"

"Yes. We'll all come with you."

Sebastian's face crumples up like confused laundry.

"Who's 'we'?"

"We," the troll repeats.

When Sebastian looks out over the beach he sees a hundred thousand trolls.

"Who are they?"

The troll hugs Sebastian until Sebastian is only hugging air. The other trolls walk toward him and disappear, one by one, all through the same crack. But they call out from the inside:

"We're the voices in your head that tell you not to do

it, Sebastian. When the others say 'jump,' 'stop swimming,' and 'set fire to the rope.' We're the ones that tell you not to."

Sebastian looks at his hands. One of the cracks closes up. Then another one. He holds the invisible scars against his cheek and wonders how you live with them instead of living in them. Then he closes his eyes again, sleeps all night there in the sand.

He dreams. Not that he's running, like he usually does. Not that he's falling or drowning. He dreams that he's climbing now, up a rope, to the top of a cliff. When he wakes up, he's on his own next to the hole. He drops the rope and it falls to the bottom, lands with a soft thud. Far down there in the sand, the boy can still read what the troll wrote when it said, "Just be," and the boy said, "Be what?"

It says *Sebastian*. Just that.

He sits with his feet dangling over the edge and awaits the sound of rain against the roof of the bubble.

But nothing comes, and far away he sees something else, something he hasn't seen in so long, he's forgotten what it looks like. A line in the sky, from top to bottom. Sebastian has to turn his head to the side until his neck sounds like bubble wrap before he finally realizes what it is.

A crack in the glass. Just the one. He can barely fit his hand through it. His mother touches his fingertips on the other side. He hears her shout his name into the bubble, and he whispers:

"You don't have to scream, Mom . . . I . . . can hear you."

"Sebastian . . ." she whispers then, the way only the person who gave a child its name can whisper it.

"Yes, Mom," he replies.

"What can I do for you?" she sobs.

Sebastian thinks for a long time before he finally answers:

"Breakfast. I'd like . . . breakfast."

When his mother whispers that she loves him, snow starts falling from the sky. But when it lands inside the bubble it's not frozen flakes, it's freshly shed fur, small bits of fluffy fuzz that settle softly on Sebastian's skin. It's still early, maybe he doesn't have words for this yet, but in time he might be able to talk about it. One day when someone says something and maybe he laughs for the first time. Or when he laughs as if it were the first time, over and over again. Laughs as if someone a very, very long time ago found the laugh on the ground in a forest, broken to pieces after a storm, and brought it home and nursed it until the laugh was strong enough to be released into the wild again. And then it takes off from the rooftops, straight up towards the heavens, as though someone let go of a balloon to make it happy. Maybe, in a hundred thousand years.

He blinks at the light, as the sunrise gently tugs at the clouds until the night lets go. There's a note in his pocket. He'll find it soon.

Don't jump, it says, written with someone's most beautiful letters.

> *don't jump*
> *sebastian please*
> *don't jump*
> *because we really really want to know*
> *who you can become*
> *if you don't.*

Just that.

ACKNOWLEDGMENTS

would like to thank all the very nice people who have been patient enough to read everything I've written over the years. Even the weird stuff. It's been a great and overwhelming ride.

These three stories in particular were never really meant to be a book, so I would like to thank my publisher for making it into one anyway. Especially Brendan May, Kevin Hanson, and Rita Silva, whose belief in me and my writing has really been quite unreasonable.

Furthermore, I would like to say thanks to my wife, as always. You're my castle. Whenever I'm with you I'm safe.

Thanks also to Tor Jonasson and Marie Gyllenhammar at Salomonsson Agency, for keeping it all together, and for sticking by me. It's not always been easy, I'm aware of that.

A final shoutout to my grandmother, who was always my toughest critic and biggest fan. I'm still trying to make you proud. And to the friends I lost along the way, some because of disease and some because of pain: I really miss you guys.

Fredrik Backman

Fredrik Backman is the *New York Times* bestselling author of *A Man Called Ove*, *My Grandmother Asked Me to Tell You She's Sorry*, *Britt-Marie Was Here*, *Beartown*, and *Us Against You*. His books have been published in more than thirty-five countries. He lives in Stockholm, Sweden, with his wife and two children.

Also by

FREDRIK BACKMAN

Internationally Bestselling Author

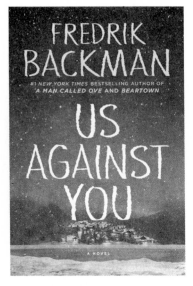

"This is a story about
people—about strength
and tribal loyalty."

Jojo Moyes,
New York Times bestselling author
of *Me Before You*

"Fredrik Backman is one of
the world's best and most
interesting novelists."

Washington Times

SIMON &
SCHUSTER
CANADA